POOH!

Collect all the Preston Pig Stories

Colin McNaughton
Suddenly!

Colin McNaughton
GOAL!

Colin McNaughton
BOO!

Colin McNaughton
Shh!
(Don't Tell Mister Wolf)
A Preston Pig Lift-the-Flap Book

Colin McNaughton
Oops!

Colin McNaughton
Hmm...
A Preston Pig Story

Colin McNaughton
Hawoo!
A Preston Pig Story

Coming soon!

First published in Great Britain by HarperCollins Publishers in 2001

1 3 5 7 9 10 8 6 4 2

ISBN: 0 00 712370 1

From the television series based on the original Preston Pig books created, written and illustrated by Colin McNaughton

Text © Colin McNaughton/HarperCollins Publishers Ltd 2001

Illustrations in this work derived from the television series © Colin McNaughton/Varga-London Ltd 1999

Production of the television series by Varga-London Ltd and Link Entertainment; Licensed by Link Licensing Ltd

The author/illustrator asserts the moral right to be identified as the author/illustrator of the work.

A CIP catalogue record for this title is available from the British Library.

The HarperCollins website address is: www.**fire**and**water**.com

Printed in Hong Kong

Colin McNaughton
POOH!

Collins

An imprint of HarperCollinsPublishers

Mister Wolf is babysitting.

"Ga...ga...goo!" coos the baby.

"Grr! I hate babies!" mutters Mister Wolf.

Some passers-by stop to look in the pram.

"**Pooh!**" say the passers-by.

"**POOH!**" says Mister Wolf. "This is *so* embarrassing."

Meanwhile, at Preston's house, Preston has an important question.
"Mum," says Preston, "where do babies come from?"
"Ah...er...um...ask your father," says Preston's mum.

"Dad," says Preston, "where do babies come from?"

"Did you ask your mother?" says Preston's dad.

"Yes," says Preston, "she said to ask *you*."

"Oh, well...ah...yes...er...um... they grow under...er...um... gooseberry bushes!" says Preston's dad.

Mister Wolf is pushing the baby past Preston's house when he spies a bush.

"Hmm...I'll just leave you here," says Mister Wolf to the baby. "Won't be long."

The baby makes a noise from its bottom. Parp!

"**Pooh!**" says Mister Wolf.

Preston goes looking for a gooseberry bush and finds one. He looks underneath it and sees...a pram!

"A baby," whispers Preston. "Dad was right!
I'll take it to the park."

At the park Preston meets Billy the Bully.

"What's in the pram, Preston?" says Billy the Bully. "A dolly? Preston's got a dolly!"

"Wah!" cries the baby.

"It's not a dolly, it's a baby," says Preston crossly, "and you've woken him up!"

Nearby, Mister Wolf hears the noisy baby.

"Hmm…so Preston's babysitting too!" says Mister Wolf. "Yum, yum! Roast Preston and suckling pig! Maybe I *do* like babies, after all!"

Down at the duck pond the baby is crying again.
"**Pooh!**" says Mister Plump the park keeper.
"His nappy needs changing."
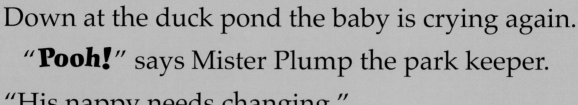
Preston takes a good sniff and says,
"**Pooh!** I think you might have
a point there," and he whips
off the baby's nappy.
"**POOH!**" says
Mister Wolf.

Preston wheels the pram over the bridge.

"Wah!" cries the baby.

"What now?" says Preston.

"Wah! Wah!" cries the baby.

"He wants his dummy," says Mister Plump
the park keeper.

Mister Wolf is lurking under the water.
The baby spits out the dummy. It flies through the
air and lands right in Mister Wolf's snorkel.

"Wah!" cries the baby.
"Where's your
dummy?" says Preston.

Mister Wolf blows
through the
snorkel. Whee!...
the dummy flies out and lands straight back in
the baby's mouth.
"You've found it! Well done!" says Preston.

Mister Wolf staggers out of the pond and steps
on Mister Plump's rake. **SMACK!**

"Ow!" says Mister Wolf. "That really hurt!"

"Wah! Wah! Wah!" cries the baby.
"What is it *now*?" says Preston crossly.
"He's hungry," says Mister Plump.
"Give him his bottle, then come over here.
I've got a little plant for your mum."

Preston gives the baby his bottle, then goes to see Mister Plump.

"Mmm!" says Mister Wolf, licking his lips. "Fresh piglet!"

"Burp!" says the baby.

"**Pooh!**" chokes Mister Wolf.

Preston comes back with the plant from Mister Plump.

"Wah! Mamma! Mamma!" yells the baby.

"It's time *you* went back under the gooseberry bush!" says Preston. "I've had enough of babies. They're noisy, they've got no manners and they stink!"

"Shh!" whispers Preston to the baby. "Don't wake Billy the Bully!"

"Wah!" cries the baby, quietly.

Suddenly, the baby's bottle flies out of the pram and bonks Billy the Bully on the nose.

"Oi! Who did that?" yells Billy the Bully. "You!"
Billy the Bully points at Mister Wolf.

"B-b-but!" cries Mister Wolf. "It wasn't me!
I can explain..."

Preston puts the baby back under the gooseberry bush. Just then, he sees his friend Pumpkin.

"Have a smell of these flowers, Pumpkin," says Preston.

"**Pooh!**" says Pumpkin. "They smell like a baby's bottom!"

They wander off, laughing.

Mister Wolf hobbles back to the pram.
"Just as well I didn't take you to the park,"
says Mister Wolf. "It's far too dangerous."
As Mister Wolf is lifting the baby out of
the pram, the baby
bites his nose.
"**Ow!**" says Mister Wolf.
"That hurt! That
really hurt!"

Then Mister Wolf feels something
oozing through his fingers.
"Oh, **Pooh!**" howls Mister Wolf.
"I hate babies."

THE END